Lisa Kopelke

The Younger Brother's SURVIVAL GUIDE

by Matt

Simon & Schuster Books for Young Readers
NEW YORK LONDON TORONTO SYDNEY

SIMON & SCHUSTER BOOKS FOR YOUNG READERS
An imprint of Simon & Schuster Children's Publishing Division
1230 Avenue of the Americas, New York, New York 10020

Book design by Dan Potash
The text for this book is set in Coop Forged.
The illustrations for this book are rendered in acrylic and mixed media.
Manufactured in Mexico
2 4 6 8 10 9 7 5 3 1
Library of Congress Cataloging-in-Publication Data • Kopelke, Lisa.
The younger brother's survival guide : by Matt / Lisa Kopelke.— 1st ed. • p. cm.
Summary: Matt presents some tips on how to survive being
a younger brother to a sometimes tricky older sister.
ISBN-13: 978-0-689-86249-6 (hardcover)
ISBN-10: 0-689-86249-0
[1. Brothers and sisters—Fiction.] I. Title.
PZ7.K83614Yo 2005
[E]—dc22 2004012629

To Claire

Thank you, Matt!

It's not easy having an older sister. That's why I wrote THE YOUNGER BROTHER'S SURVIVAL GUIDE. Here it is (and don't show it to your sister!).

My sister likes to make her favorite treat for us, Mystery Shake.

For some reason mine always tastes funny.

This brings me to
Tip #1:
Switch glasses when
she's not looking.

My sister and I eat a ton of candy.
She gets me to experiment with mine.

Tip #2:
Don't listen to your sister if she tells you to stick candy up your nose.

And

Tip #3:

Don't try to get the candy out of your nose with bubble gum, even if she swears it'll work.

My parents say my sister and I run around the house like wild animals.

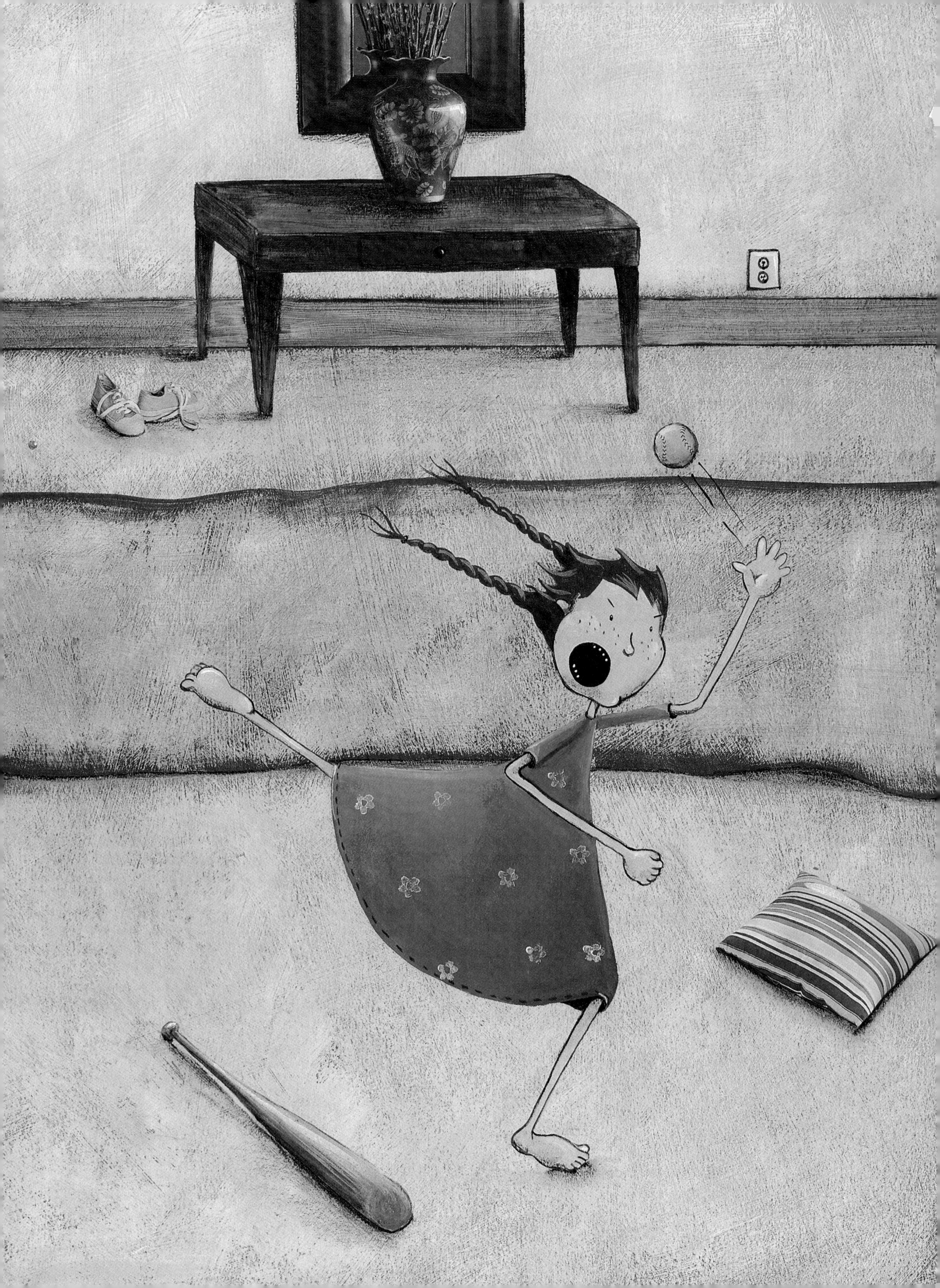

Tip #4:
Never run around the house in your underwear—just in case your sister locks you outside.

My sister likes to dress me up and take pictures.
She shows them to all her friends.

Tip #5:
Just go along.
There are some things
you have to put up with.

Besides, you can take funnier pictures of HER later.

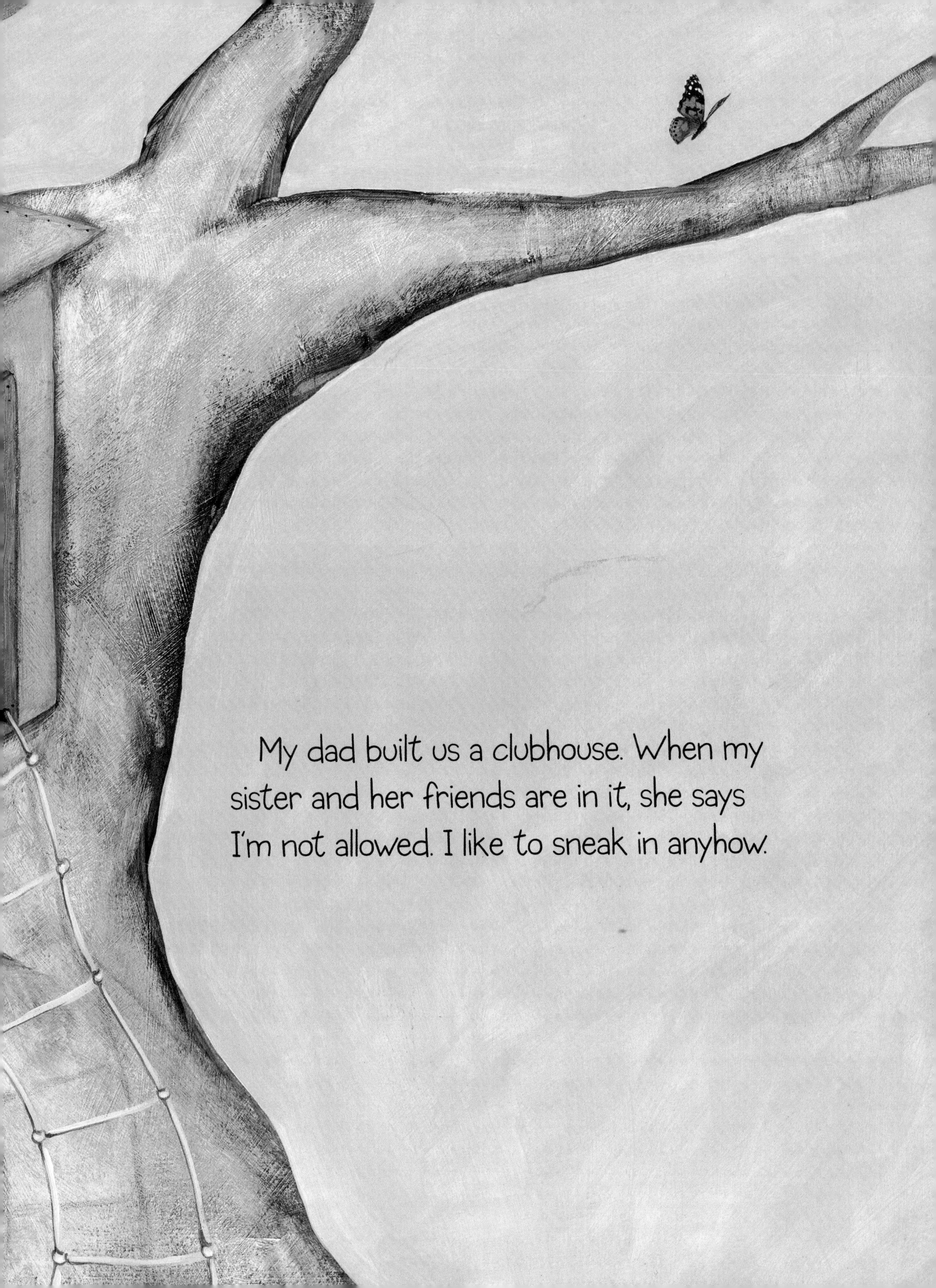

My dad built us a clubhouse. When my sister and her friends are in it, she says I'm not allowed. I like to sneak in anyhow.

Tip #6:
If you don't want your sister
to hear you, don't tie a rope
around your waist and jump
off the deck, even if you are
a superhero.

Today my sister went to summer camp for a whole week. I enjoy doing nice things for her while she's away to show her how much I miss her.

Tip #7:
Be sure to show off your creative skills by redecorating everything in your sister's room.

Finally,
Tip #8:
Ride away really fast when your sister finds out what you've done.

It's not always easy having an older sister,
but it's always an adventure.